Rachel Moss (illustrator) is a graphic designer in love with the bright colors and vibrant energy of the Caribbean. She was born in Jamaica and studied animation in England at the University for the Creative Arts. Moss now lives in Jamaica where she spends her days illustrating children's books such as *I Am a Promise* by Shelly Ann Fraser Pryce, *Abigail's Glorious Hair,* and *Milo & Myra Learn Manners with Mr. Mongoose.*

"African"
Song written by Peter Tosh
Courtesy of Irving Music Inc. on behalf of Number Eleven Music
Used by Permission. All Rights Reserved.

LyricPop is a children's picture book collection by LyricVerse and Akashic Books.

lyricverse.

Published by Akashic Books
Song lyrics ©1977 Peter Tosh
Illustrations ©2020 Rachel Moss

ISBN: 978-1-61775-799-0
Library of Congress Control Number: 2019947939
First printing

Printed in Malaysia

Akashic Books
Brooklyn, New York, USA
Ballydehob, Co. Cork, Ireland
Twitter: @AkashicBooks
Facebook: AkashicBooks
E-mail: info@akashicbooks.com
Website: www.akashicbooks.com

African

Song Lyrics by Peter Tosh
Illustrations by Rachel Moss

Don't care where you
come from,
as long as you're a
black man,

you're an African

No mind your nationality,
you have got the identity of an

African

'Cause if you come from Clarendon
(You are an African)

And if you come from Portland
(You are an African)

And if you come from Westmoreland,
you're an African

So don't care where
you come from,
as long as you're a
black man,
you're an African

No mind your nationality,
you have got the identity of an

African

'Cause if you come from Trinidad
(You are an African)

And if you come from Nassau

(You are an African)

And if you come from Cuba,

you are an African

So don't care where you come from,
as long as you're a black man,
you're an African

No mind your complexion,
there is no rejection,
you're an African

'Cause if your 'plexion high, high, high,
if your 'plexion low, low,
and if your 'plexion in between,

you're an African

So don't care
where you come from,
as long as you're a black man,
you're an African

No mind denomination,
that is only segregation,

you're an African

'Cause if you go to the Catholic

(You are an African)

And if you go to the Methodist

(You are an African)

And if you go to the Church of Gods,

you're an African

So don't care where you come from,
as long as you're a black man,
you're an African

No mind your nationality,
you have got the identity of an
African

'Cause if you come from Brixton

(You are an African)

And if you come from Neasden
(You are an African)

And if you come from Willesden
(You are an African)

And if you come from Bronx

(You are an African)

And if you come from Brooklyn

(You are an African)

And if you come from Queens

(You are an African)

And if you come from Manhattan

(You are an African)

And if you come from Canada

(You are an African)

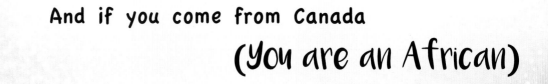

And if you come from Miami

(You are an African)

And if you come from Switzerland

(You are an African)

And if you come
from Germany
(You are an African)

And if you come from Russia

(You are an African)

And if you come from Taiwan

(You are an African)

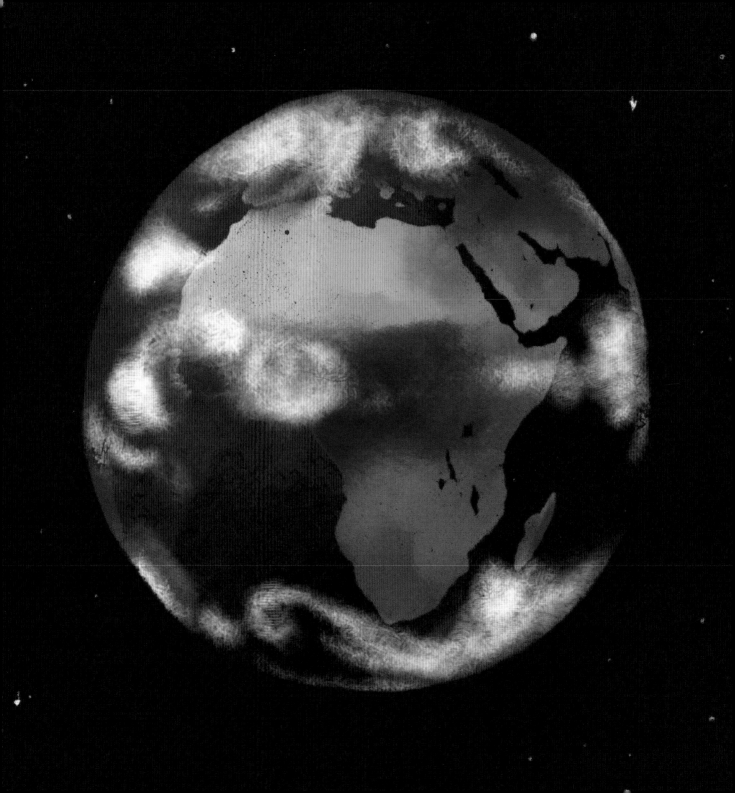

Also available from **LyricPop**

GOOD VIBRATIONS
Song lyrics by Mike Love and Brian Wilson
Illustrations by Paul Hoppe
Mike Love and Brian Wilson's world-famous song, gloriously illustrated by Paul Hoppe, will bring smiles to the faces of children and parents alike.
Hardcover, $16.95, ISBN: 978-1-61775-787-7 | E-book, $16.99, 978-1-61775-833-1

WE'RE NOT GONNA TAKE IT
Song lyrics by Dee Snider
Illustrations by Margaret McCartney
A playful picture book echoing 1980s hair band Twisted Sister's most popular antiestablishment anthem.
Hardcover, $16.95, ISBN: 978-1-61775-788-4 | E-book, $16.99, 978-1-61775-834-8

DON'T STOP
Song lyrics by Christine McVie
Illustrations by Nusha Ashjaee
A beautifully illustrated picture book based on Christine McVie of Fleetwood Mac's enduring anthem to optimism and patience.
Hardcover, $16.95, ISBN: 978-1-61775-805-8 | E-book, $16.99, 978-1-61775-831-7